CH00853476

My Daddy is a Monster

The second title in the **Monstrous Me Collection**

Written by Natalie Reeves Billing

Illustrated by Lisa Williams

Dedicated to Daddy Billing, more monster than man, but we love him. And to all the long-suffering daddy monsters of our world. It does get easier ... I think.

Acknowledgements

Thank you for coming with me on this journey, and making my Monstrous Me Collection a reality. Big love to my family, Billing and Reeves. How do you put up with me? To Colin, Greg, Meg, Nathaniel, Ellie Rose and Scooblet. Mum, Christie, Matt, Marquise, Sarayah and Uncle Billy. And to my crazy ozzie dad with the weird hair.

Thanks to my soul sisters, Julie, Lynn, Sue, Klare, Tegan, and Angelas: Churm and Basford. Also, the ladies of Team Author, Sue Miller, Lisa Williams, Sarah Fountain and Jude Lennon. Without you, none of this would be possible. And to the legend that is Rebecca McComb, thanks for keeping me social.

And to my soul bros: Totti, Alex, and Paul with the cheese and wine.

Praise to the institutions that are The Women's Org, Ali and Jacqueline and all the crew. SSE, Lisa and the start-up crew. Writing on the Wall. You guys bring the magic.

To my Insta, Twitter and FB peeps, and to you the reader. Without you, none of it works. You're all totally Roarsome!

Monstrometer

This pesky Monstrometer has a habit of getting lost. Can you find one in each picture?

My Daddy is a Monster
My Kids are Monsters

By Natalie Reeves Billing

Illustrated by Lisa Williams

Book 2 in the Monstrous Me Collection

First published in 2020

Copyright Natalie Reeves Billing © 2020
All rights reserved.

ISBN 978-1-9163889-3-2

The rights of the author and illustrator have been asserted in accordance with Sections 77 and 78 of the Copyright Designs and Patents Act, 1988.

No part of this book or its illustrations may be reproduced (including photocopying or storing in any medium by electronic means and whether or not transiently or incidentally to some other use of this publication) without the written permission of the copyright holder except in accordance with the provisions of the Copyright, Design and Patents Act 1988.

PERSPECTIVZ

LOLLIPOP LODGE

TEAM AUTHOR UK
Publishing with you

About the Monstrous Me Collection

The Monstrous Me Collection is a series of split perspective books. Their aim is to look at situations from multiple points of view, helping children develop a sense of balance, roundedness and wellbeing. Children can literally and figuratively, turn the story on its head, and look at the very same situations from different angles.

The Monstrous Me Collection is a fun, multi-layered reading experience for all the family. When you've finished reading, why not try to find the hidden Monstrometers? A Monstrometer is a magical, mirror-like machine that can detect if someone truly is a monster. There's one on every page.

Look out for other titles in the Monstrous Me Collection:

Titles by the same author and illustrator:

About the Author

Natalie Reeves Billing is a Liverpool girl with a wicked sense of humour. She spent her early years in the music industry as a singer/songwriter. This led to storytelling.

Natalie is a fellow of the School of Social Entrepreneurs under the Lloyds Bank program, and a member of the Golden Egg Academy. Her poetry and stories are published in several anthologies.

www.lollipoplodge.net

About the Illustrator

Lisa Williams decided to be an illustrator whilst she was still in primary school. She has been illustrating children's books, magazines and educational material for nearly 25 years. Whilst taking on commercial work, Lisa took a teacher training course, but since qualifying, her commercial success has been such that she hasn't had the time to teach! Lisa is one of the talented illustrators for Team Author UK. This allows her to work with a variety of authors and the opportunity to develop an array of styles.

For more information, visit Lisa's Facebook page:

🇫 @lisawilliamsillustration

My daddy's a monster, but no one can see,
And nobody knows but my sister and me.
We told Mum, but she said she already knew.
We've always suspected that Mum is one, too.

No one else knows because monsters can hide,
And lots of dads have monsters hidden inside.
Would you like to know how children can tell
If Daddykins is a real monster as well?

Just before daybreak, I hear a big noise,
My dad is outside and he's breaking my toys.
That tower had taken a whole day to make
But only a second for Daddy to break.

My daddy can't wait to get us to school,
He drives a big truck, and he thinks that he's cool.
He straps us in tight so we can't touch his seats,
And he's stopped us from laughing and
eating our sweets.

BOA VISTA PRIMARY

ALTERNIA POINT

When Dad makes the dinner, it's 'No iPad' time,
"The boss of our country should make that a crime!"

But, here is Dad's phone!
It's got games and all sorts.
I find some nice pictures of
Dad in his shorts.

SHARE

Dad gives us something disgusting for dinner,
I think it's because he's been trying to get thinner.
For who'd want to eat a potato in skin?
And carrots are best when they're chucked in a bin.

He drags us to watch muddy men kick a ball,
Though, my sister and I have no interest at all.
We can't play our games, we have nothing to eat,
And my bum is so cold on this hard, plastic seat.

But then, when he puts me to bed in the night,
Ruffles my hair just to check I'm all right,
Tells me nice things, that I'm clever and tall,
Then I wonder if my dad's a monster at all!

Did you find those pesky Monstrometers?
Monstrometers help us see the monsters all around us.

Can you make your book somersault? Close the book, and
give it a flip, and let's read from a different point of view.

Did you find those pesky Monstrometers?
Monstrometers help us see the monsters all around us.

Can you make your book somersault? Close the book, and
give it a flip, and let's read from a different point of view.

But, when I look in on them every night,
And ruffle their fur just to check they're all right,
I see them both smiling, so peaceful and small.
Then, I wonder if my kids are monsters at all!

They grumble and say that there's nothing to do,
She's hungry and cold, and my son needs a poo.

We go to the game to
see Honeywell score

Like my father, my gramps,
and his father before.

I lay out the table with potatoes and ham,
Though my son wants pizza, my daughter wants jam.
I've also made carrots and warm chicken strips,
But my son prefers noodles, my daughter likes chips.

I'm making the dinner. The kids are alone,
I don't even notice they've stolen my phone.
I get loads of calls from my uncles and aunts
To tell me they love my new Valentine's pants.

At school time, I hurry them into the truck,
They fidget, and fight and the seatbelts get stuck.
I see my son chewing, but what's there to eat?
He found an old crisp down the back of his seat.

I get up real early to warm up the house,
And creep past their bedrooms as quiet as a mouse.
A pain in my foot makes me scream, makes me snort,
But they only care that I've broken their fort!

No one else knows because monsters can hide,
Even sweet children have monsters inside.
Do you know how worried daddies can tell
If their little angels are monsters as well?

My children are monsters that no one can see,
And, nobody knows except Mummy and me.
I told Gran, but she said she already knew,
I've always suspected that she's monstrous too!

MY KIDS ARE MONSTERS

Second title in the **Monstrous Me Collection**

Written by Natalie Reeves Billing

Illustrated by Lisa Williams

Look out for the
Monstrometers in
every picture!